"Today's Struggles Is Tomorrow's Strength"

Written By : Christopher C. Smith

2

Christopher C. Smith
Father, Author, Actor, Independent Publisher & Song Writer

With much gratitude and many thanks to 1st Born (President of Iron Fist Global), Benjamin Brothers and Associates, and many others
"The Original Hip Hop Shop" is back again for the first time! Although located in the exact location as Maurice Malone's Hip Hop Shop, which closed in 1998, The Original Hip Hop Shop is NOT affiliated with Malone.
The grand opening started with a 21 Mic Salute honoring DeShaun Dupree Holton aka Big Proof on October 2nd, 2014, which also happens to be Proofs birthday.
We are committed to preserving the Culture while dedicating honors to the memory of Iconic Legends of Hip Hop creating "Opportunities within its Community" for aspiring artists to pursue their entrepreneurial dreams.

Thank you's

First I would like to give thanks to god

My Beautiful Mother
Ora Henderson

My Beautiful Daughter
Lauren Madison Smith

My supportive family, MarQuetta Davis, Kendra Davis, Juan Burgin Jr. ,Rae Shawn Burgin, Ophelia Smith, Angela Williams,
My Beautiful sister Valerie Hayes ,My niece Valyn, My nephews Vashon and D.J., Raquel Martinez & Debbie, Juju & Mia, Neme Cancel & The Entire Point Blank Fam Inc., Cash Blocka & the B.G.G, Damarkus Christmas Darrell Washington, Christopher Bullock, D.J. Speak Eazy & G-Five, Hell Rell & the Whole Top Gunnas Family, The whole Yonkers & Bronx Family, Moe Dirdee, 1st Born, Nikki & Amy, My whole Detroit Family, Aggie & Every Body at the Wal-Mart #5404 Store

BIG THANKS TO SHACORA JOHNSON

Table of Contents

Thank you's   Page 5

Chapter 1   Page 8

Chapter 2   Page 15

Chapter 3   Page 23

Chapter 4   Page 30

Poems   Page 37

Special thanks to Raquel, Juju & Mia

THANKS FOR ALL YOUR LOVE AND SUPPORT

Chapter 1

"ALLLLL RISE!" The bailiff yelled at the top of his lungs while the judge slowly entered the room and took his seat from coming back from a brief 15 minute break.

While slowly getting up I took a deep breath and as I began to stand, I couldn't help but take a gentle glimpse of my son, Joseph. He held his head down as if he was just as nervous as me. Only, he was sitting on the opposite side of the court room.

"Good morning," the Judge said while putting his glasses on his face. As he began to read the papers that were placed on his bench he spoke again, "Why should I grant you *your* wish of giving you *your* son back, Mrs. Davis, with all that he has been through at such a young age while being in your custody?"

With a straight face, I began to stutter, "Your honor, I'm doing a lot better than

I was at the time." My voice began to crack while trying to hold back from crying,

"I'm finally in a home of my own and I am currently working two jobs while attending online classes to get my G.E.D".

"Well, after hearing both sides," he said calmly while giving me straight eye to eye contact, "and seeing that you, Mrs. Davis, has met the requirements that were given at the last court date—I hereby grant you full custody of your son, Joseph Davis".

"Oh my God! Thank you, Jesus!" I said with an emotional outburst as tears began to fill my eyes and quickly fall from the cheeks of my face.

"Thank you so much, Judge!" I said while looking over at Joseph to see his response.

"Court is adjourned," the Judge said while slamming his gavel on his desk.

I quickly began to pack up all my belongings while talking to my lawyer

Valerie who represented me throughout the case.

"You are the best," I said with a smile, giving her the tightest hug.

"No problem," she slowly replied while wiping tears from her eyes, "Look who is behind you," she said with a smirk on her face.

With a confused look I felt a soft tap and heavy breathing on my shoulder. It was Joseph.

"Hi Mom, I missed you," he started to break down and cry.

I could not help but hug and hold him while whispering in his ear, "It's going to be okay." I wiped the tears from his eyes and looked deeply into his face and said, "You're coming back home now... and I've missed you too."

From the way he was dressed you could tell he was not eating much or being treated properly. He stood five feet nine inches and look as if like he only weighed one hundred and twenty-nine pounds.

As we headed out of the court room Joseph began to narrate all of the trials and tribulations he experienced while staying at his Aunt Jasmine's house. Ironically, this was the same person who's jealously and necessity to have everything I had landed me in court in the first place. The stories seemed to never end so interrupted him, "No more looking back son" I said. "The plate is clean and from now on we will be looking ahead and just let the past be the past".

"I'm hungry mom," he said gently as we walked toward the car.

"What would you like to…?" was all I could ask before being interrupted.

"Anything!" Joseph blurted out jokingly. I did not mind though because it made it incredibly easy for us to settle on a drive-thru

As we circled through the parking lot to order our food I could not help but just look at Joseph with a smile. Thinking to myself—wow, it's really been seven *long* years since I've had my son living with me.

"So, how's school going for you?" I said while pulling up to the window to get the food that I had ordered.

"School's fine, Mom. Just having a little trouble here and there."

A nervous facial expression came over my face as I slowly began to pull off and looked at Joseph, "What do you mean trouble?" I asked.

"Well I had been having trouble with this one gang at my school. They call themselves *The Almighty Smith Gang* or just *A.S.G.*"

"Did you need me to come up there or get the cops involved?" I said anxiously.

Joseph instantly swept the suggestion aside. "No. Thanks Ma! I can handle it on my own. It's really nothing to worry about."

Feeling exhausted and tired, we finally arrived at my house—*our* house. However, a sigh of relief came over me as we walked toward the house together.

"Well! Son, this is your new home!" I exclaimed with a bright smile on my face.

As we entered the house, I couldn't help but notice the overwhelming look on Joseph's face as he examined his new space and looked around at the different pictures and paintings I had of him while he was a baby.

"Wow! Mom, I remember taking this picture" he said while taking a deep breath and picking up one of the big pictures I had of me and him hanging on the wall.

"Aww yeah! Those were the days but you're all grown up now and in high school" I jokingly replied while trying to hold back my tears.

"Well son, I will show you your bedroom now. It's almost time to go to bed for school tomorrow," I said with a more serious look on my face.

"Ok, thanks ma! This is a beautiful house you have."

"Thanks Jay! Well," I said standing in his room door, "I will talk to you in the morning. We both have a busy day ahead of us" I said, closing his door.

It had been a long, eventful day and it was finally time to rest my head. While lying down I could not help but break down in tears and prayerfully thank God for answering my previous prayers.

For God had finally returned my son home to me safe and sound.

Chapter 2

I felt uneasy pulling into the driveway of my house after dropping Joseph off at school. For some reason, *something* just did not feel right.

"What's up, punk?"

Juan, one of the leaders from the A.S.G., was angry. He swung and hit me in the back of my head before I could attempt to turn around and see who was talking.

"Get up! Get up now, chump!" Juan said as he continued to pound on me causing my face to hit the lockers.

I balled up in the corner of the walls. "Stop! Stop, stop!" I yelled while other students began to crowd around us to see what the commotion was about.

"Fight! Fight! Fight!" The crowd chanted as I got up. I tried to swing back but fell short of hitting Juan's face.

For this, other members of the Smith Gang began to jump in as a pool of my blood began to fill the school's hall.

"Stop it! Stop, leave him alone! Leave him alone!" A loud cry echoed out of the crowd seeming to get closer. It was a girl. "Leave him alone, you little punk", she uttered aggressively, pushing Juan and others away from me.

"Are you okay?" she questioned. "Hey? Are you okay?"

I attempted to get myself together as she spoke again, "Hi, my name is Kendra. Here, take my scarf and cover yourself. You'll need it.

"They got you pretty bad," Kendra said with a serious tone while nursing my injuries. "Oh my God! I can't *believe* they did this to you! What's your name anyway?"

"My name is Joseph", I replied while fixing myself up to act as if nothing ever happened. Only, my eye was swollen and barely opened. As I went to touch my face, blood leaked down into his hands. "Ouch!"

The crowd that once filled the halls was small now that the bell rang to start the next period's class.

"Can you please help me to the nurse's office?" I asked Kendra.

"No problem", she replied while picking up all my belongings and making sure nothing was left behind.

"Here, let's stop by the restroom to rinse you off," Kendra said as she guided me through the school. Somehow I managed to see my busted lip through my swollen left eye in the bathroom mirror's reflection; my face was messed up.

Finally, we made it to the nurse's office and I filled out the sign-in sheet. Each student stared at my injuries as they exited the infirmary, it made hard to concentrate. They all seemed shocked to see that I survived the fight. For that same reason, Juan visited the nurse's office. He stared dead at me through the glass windows signaling what looked like an alert for me better not snitch.

Feeling uncomfortable, I put my focus back on signing in. "Are you ok?" Kendra spoke. She looked around and seen Juan in the hall. "Don't worry about him he likes intimidating people just to do it. There is nothing to worry about. You stood your ground and didn't run. That's all that matters."

"Yeah, you're right," I replied. "But still, how do I explain a swollen eye, a busted lip and these scratches to my Mom?"

"Now that, you're on your own!" Kendra replied jokingly.

But I wasn't. I planned to go straight home and ice my eye. With everything that happened I just wanted to fall asleep and hope for a better day tomorrow. But as soon as I put the key through the door my mom was on me.

As soon as I turned the knob on the front door she was sitting on the living room couch with her hands crossed, waiting anxiously.

"Joseph, are you okay? What happened?" Tears streamed from her eyes as seen me. "Oh my god! I'm about to call the police."

"Mom! Please don't!" I begged. "It will only make it worst. Just, please Mom! It's nothing!"

"Son, what do you mean? You look a hot mess," she replied. "How did this all happen?" she questioned.

"Mom, I have no idea. It all just happened out the blue but luckily my friend Kendra was there to help me out and make sure I got cleaned up"

She held her head low then began to pray. "Oh God! In Jesus' name, oh Lord! You know I don't need this right now with all that I'm going through.

"Son, I brought you here and fought for you to come here and live a better life. I didn't want you to have to go through this at all."

"I know, Mom, but please! The last thing I want is for you to stress out about it. It's just a few minor cuts," I pleaded, "I will survive".

I walked away, up the stairs, into my bedroom where I politely slammed the door and tried to fall asleep. Only to have my cell phone wake me right back up with text messages and phone calls from random people checking up on me to make sure that everything was okay.

"You okay?" Kendra asked. "How did your mom take it?"

"No lie, she freaked out", I said jokingly she even offered to call the police and try to get Juan and the Smith Gang arrested. I told her not to though because that would only bring more drama and make matters worse. But thanks again for being there for me. I think the fight would've still been going on had you not been there," I said with a small chuckle. "But enough about me how was your day?"

"Well, it was fine," Kendra replied "I just got off the phone with my girlfriend".

"Your *girlfriend*?" I said with a shocked face. My mouth dropped.

"Yes, my girlfriend!" Kendra said with a serious tone. "We have been dating for a few months now. She was there while you were getting your ass whooped," Kendra joked. "In fact she was the one who had let me know what was going on."

"That's cool. Hey, to each its own! I'm not the one to judge," I said with a blank stare on my face. Then we both were silent for 2 minutes. "Well! I will see you tomorrow at school. It's getting a little late and I have to shower and eat dinner."

"That's fine, I was just checking up on you", Kendra last spoke, "give me a call if you need anything!"

"Okay thanks! I will keep that in mind. Once again, thanks for being there."

I hung up the phone and my mom entered the room.

"Are you okay?" she asked with a very concerned look.

I took a deep breath and said, "Yeah, I'm fine."

"Well dinner will be ready in couple of minutes, so make sure you finish your home work and put some more ice on that eye to stop the swelling."

That night after finishing dinner, as I headed back to my room I couldn't help but notice small cries I heard from my mom as she tiredly washed the dishes. I held my head low as I continued up the stairs. Hearing my Mom's pain I began to feel ashamed. I could not do this anymore; this is embarrassing.

Chapter 3

RING, RING, RING!!!

My alarm went off and I sluggishly got ready for school. When I came down the stairs my mom had already left for work. While heading out the back door I noticed a small note that she wrote stating that she left a few dollars for me for lunch and that she loved me.

"Be safe" the note read.

I started to continue out of the back door when a small pocket knife lying by the kitchen sink caught my attention.

I thought to myself, if I take this, what happened yesterday won't happen *ever* again. So I quickly grabbed the knife along with the cash and headed toward the bus stop.

While standing with the other kids waiting to go to school, I seen Kendra and her girlfriend hugging.

"Hey what's up?" I said while still yawning from waking up.

"What's wrong, I see someone didn't get enough sleep last night" Kendra said sarcastically.

"I did. It's just that I'm not a morning person. By the way, how does my eye look?" I slightly rubbed the small bruise.

"It's still there but not as bad as it once was," Kendra replied.

We reached school and I was heading toward my 1st period class when I saw Juan and the Smith Gang posted by the lockers as if they had nowhere to go. I thought to myself, do not mind them, and just continue walking. I kept walking with my head held low as if I was invincible.

"What's up Joseph, let me talk to you," Juan said.

Without replying, I walked into my class like I didn't hear anything.

"So you're just going to ignore me, Joseph?" Juan said, while looking through the glass window of the class room as if he was trying to taunt and intimidate me.

Ring, ring, ring! **The bell rang and class had started.**

"So kids how was your day" my teacher Mrs. Henderson said as she began to teach the lessons she had planned for us for the day.

As the day grew longer and school was close to ending, I became paranoid as if at any time Juan could come out of nowhere and start a fight.

When class was finally let out I went to my locker. While preparing to go home I felt a small push on my shoulder. I began to sweat with my hands in my pocket gripping on the knife I had taken from home. I quickly turned around and to my surprise it was Kendra and her girlfriend.

"Damn, you okay?" Kendra replied. "Looks like you seen a ghost," she said giggling.

"Yeah, I'm fine," I replied while feeling relieved.

"Soooo when are you going to introduce me to your Boo Thing a.k.a.

Wifey?" I said with a small smirk on my face while trying to change the subject.

"Well Joseph, this is Ashley, and Ashley, this is Joseph," Kendra said while giving Ashley a small kiss on the cheek.

"Hi, Joseph!" Ashley said while reaching her hand out to shake mines.

While doing the same I quickly replied. "HI, how are you doing?"

Before I could ask Ashley more questions I felt a hard push from behind. This time it was Juan and the Smith Gang.

"What's up, Pussy?" Juan said with that angry tone again. "What's up now?" He repeated.

"Leave him alone!" Both Ashley and Kendra yelled. "Go get a life!"

"Forget that!" Juan said. He swung and hit me up side my head. While falling and hitting my back against the locker I got into defense and started swinging back. I was getting the best of him as the whole school began to crowd around and watch. Before I knew it the whole Smith Gang had jumped in and I was getting jumped again.

26

Falling to the floor and getting back up only thing on my mind was to get to Juan and let him know that enough was enough. While punching and kicking, all I could think about is revenge

"Okay stop, stop!" Juan began to cry out. "Get him off me please, get him off of me!"

While still feeling the adrenaline rush I completely forgot that I was getting hit upside my head and kicked in my back. But the only thing that was on my mind was to get Juan and make a statement. To let him know I was not the one.

"Leave him alone!" Kendra yelled. "That's what you get Juan!"

As she tried to fight to get the guys off of me that were trying to get me off of Juan.

"Now what!" I said while punching him as hard as I possibly could. "Now what!" I repeated while sitting on top of him as he laid there helplessly on his back. I reached in my pocket and grabbed the knife I had taken from home. Opening it up and putting it to Juan's neck.

"I told you leave me alone," I said with the meanest look on my face. I looked in my face as he began to beg for his life.

"Please don't kill me! Please don't kill me," he said as tears started to fall from his eyes. Disgusted with him I got up. Kendra was still fighting and I wanted this over with.

As I ran over to break it up she stumbled and fell, hitting her head against the brick hallway walls. I immediately ran to her defense.

The crowd that once surrounded us scattered as she laid there helplessly.

"Are you okay?" Ashley and I said nervously trying to make sure she was breathing and still alive.

"Help!" Ashley screamed while lying there trying to hold Kendra's head up. "Talk to me! Talk to me!" She repeatedly!

The only thing on my mind was to hurt everyone I saw that was involved. So I began to chase down everyone I saw that played a part in the brawl. But I got halfway down the hall and seen no one I could recognize. I looked backed and stared at Kendra lying there helplessly. Teachers and Security Officers covered her as she was helped up and taken to the hospital.

"Nooo!" Ashley cried as more tears began to fall from her face.

Chapter 4

Having finally walked into the hospital, I couldn't help but break down into tears. My friend Kendra who only wanted to help me defend myself now laid there unconscious. I thought to myself, "Why God? This is all my fault."

I slowly stepped toward her bed while her girlfriend Ashley and others laid around crying, I then stood there shedding tears as I began to hold and caress her hands.

Knock, Knock!

Her doctor walked in the room holding his clipboard so close to his chest I could barely read his name badge.

"Hi, my name is Dr. Jordan," he said with a gentle but sad tone. "I will be Kendra's doctor for the time she will be here. Now, looking at her X-ray report I see that during her altercation at school she fell pretty hard, causing her to slip into a temporary coma.

"We will need her to stay here for a couple days, no more than a week to assure that she will be fine. If you guys have any questions, feel free to ask or just let me know and I will answer them."

As the doctor left the room I couldn't help but cry out. "This is all my fault!" I said repeatedly.

"No, it's not!" Ashley replied. "You guys did what you had to do to defend yourself".

"No, had I only walked away!" I replied while wiping the tears from my eyes.

"No, I'm telling you Kendra is a good friend. She will give the clothes off her back if she knows you need it. This could've happened to anyone though, it's just that it happened to her."

"Thanks!" I said, using my sleeve as a tissue.

"No problem!" Ashley said.

I stared at Kendra some more then reached over and kissed her on the cheek, just thanking her for being there for me.

Walking back in the room, with a brighter smile on his face doctor Jordan then said, "Well on brighter side, she will be waking up out of her coma in a couple days. She is able to hear everything that is going on in her surroundings."

"Ok that's fine" I tuned him out to think to myself, *Wow, this was a long day*.

"Hey, by any chance, Ashley, do you have a cell phone I can use? I need to call my mom to let her know that I'm alright and my phone died while I was on my way up here."

Ashley allowed me to use her phone. As my mom answered nervously on the first ring. I could tell she had been worrying.

"Hello, may I ask who's speaking?"

"Hi mom, it's me, Joseph."

"Oh my God! Son! Where have you been? I've been worried sick about you!" She sounded upset.

"It's been a long day," I said.

Hearing the distress in my voice she began questioning, "What's wrong? Where are you at? I'm on my way, stay there right now" She replied.

Instead of having her worry more I began to fill her in on how the day went.

"Son, I want you to know that I love you and don't want anything to happen to you. I'm on my way right now and we will talk more when we get home."

I hung up the phone, took a deep breath and glanced at Kendra as her friends and family still stood around crying and grieving. I couldn't help but feel the same way.

I finally charged my phone enough to check if I had any missed calls and texts messages.

"Look at this 37 missed calls and 14 text messages. Wow!" I said while chuckling to myself. I scanned to see exactly who called and texted me and to my surprise it was Juan. He was apologizing for the whole chaos that happened in school.

"How did he get my number in the first place?" I thought to myself. He then asked for information as to which hospital Kendra was at so he could visit and see what all was going on.

I then replied, "She is fine, just in a slight coma but is expected to make a full recovery within a couple days".

After giving him the hospital information I sat my phone to the side and continued to join her friends and family in prayers for a healthy recovery.

A couple minutes went by as we all prayed for Kendra. All in all it was not long before I noticed the door to our room slowly opening again. As I looked out the corner of my eye, I realized it was Juan.

"Wow that was fast!" I thought to myself.

The tension and discomfort that arose once Juan entered the room was undeniable. Everyone knew he was the reason Kendra was in the hospital in the first place.

"Hi, my name is Juan and I apologize for all this. I truly did not have any idea that all this would end up the way it did. I'm sorry!" The more he spoke, the more heartfelt his speech became. His voice began to crack and his eyes watered.

As Juan spoke the entire room stepped toward him and eventually comforted him. It was then that he began to cry heavily.

"Well guys I am okay though!" Kendra giggled.

We all looked over at her in shock and disbelief. She was fully awake after being in a coma. So we embraced her and became the perfect time to laugh and tell stories about the whole situation as the minutes went by.

Visiting hours finally came to an end and my mom came to pick me up. On our way home filled her in on how the whole day played out. Replaying everything made me think, "Though my struggles in life thus far were rough, with the strength and knowledge I gained from it, there is one thing I can clearly say and it is that

"Today's struggles is Tomorrow's strength"

Poems

"My Hero"
Written by Neme Cancel

3 SISTERS, TWO BROTHERS, NO FATHER
ONE MOTHER
RAISED US ALL ON HER OWN
THAT'S WHY I UNCONDITIONALLY LOVE HER
SHE KEPT A ROOF OVER OUR HEAD
AND CLOTHES ON OUR BACK
ALTHOUGH WE HAD TO SHARE BEDS
WE STILL MANAGED TO NAP
MY HERO WITHOUT A CAPE
WHO SHOWED MORE LOVE THAN HATE
EVEN WHEN TIMES WEREN'T SO GREAT
AND FOR THAT I APPRECIATE
NO SUPERWOMAN COMPARES
TO YOUR ONE OF A KIND HEART
SO BIG AND SO RARE
NO ONE CAN RIP IT APART
THERE'S NOT ENOUGH INK IN THIS PEN
NOR ENOUGH SPACE ON THIS PAD
SO
I JUST WANNA SAY THANK YOU
FOR BEING MY MOM AND MY DAD....

"A Mother's Job is never done"
Written by WINSTON NAVARRETE

A MOTHER WILL DEFEND HER CHILD TO
DEATH.
BUT THE BULLY GOT HIM UNDER STRESS.
BEING SCARED TO TELL HIS MOM WHAT'S
GOING ON. HE'S TELLING HIMSELF HE GOTTA
BE STRONG.
HIS MOTHER SEES THAT SOMETHING IS NOT
RIGHT.
IF SHE FINDS OUT SHE'S GOING ALL OUT FOR
THE FIGHT.
THE SON TELLS HER MOM I GOT A PROBLEM.
SHE SAID WHATEVER IT IS CALL ON THE LORD
& HE WILL RESOLVE IT....

www.ingramcontent.com/pod-product-compliance
Lightning Source LLC
Chambersburg PA
CBHW061504170626
46811CB00004B/1607